W9-AXL-535

THE JUNGLE BOOK

by Rudyard Kipling

#2 Rikki-Tikki-Tavi and the Mystery in the Garden

Adapted by Diane Namm

Illustrated by Jim Madsen

Sterling Publishing Co., Inc.
New York

Library of Congress Cataloging-in-Publication Data

10 9 8 7 6 5 4

Published by Sterling Publishing Co., Inc.
387 Park Avenue South, New York, NY 10016
Copyright © 2006 by Barnes and Noble, Inc.
Illustrations © 2006 by Jim Madsen
Distributed in Canada by Sterling Publishing
^{c}/o Canadian Manda Group, 165 Dufferin Street
Toronto, Ontario, Canada M6K 3H6
Distributed in the United Kingdom by GMC Distribution Services
Castle Place, 166 High Street, Lewes, East Sussex, England BN7 1XU
Distributed in Australia by Capricorn Link (Australia) Pty. Ltd.
P.O. Box 704, Windsor, NSW 2756, Australia

Printed in China

All rights reserved

Sterling ISBN 13: 978 1-4027-3290-4
        ISBN 10: 1-4027-3290-2

For information about custom editions, special sales, premium and
corporate purchases, please contact Sterling Special Sales
Department at 800-805-5489 or specialsales@sterlingpub.com.

Contents

A Turtle with No Shell

Rikki-tikki-tavi loved
to play in the garden
with the little boy, Teddy.
Teddy loved to play
with the little mongoose, too.
He also loved to eat.
   "Time for lunch,"
Teddy's mama called.

"Stay here, Rikki," Teddy said.
"Guard the house—
and stay away from
the tall, tall grass.
That is where the snakes are!"

Rikki knew he should
listen to Teddy, but
Rikki was very curious.
A little *too* curious!
He just *had* to explore
the tall, tall grass.

He had to see what was there.
Soon he saw a
very strange thing—
a creature on a rock.
"Who are you?"
Rikki asked.

"I am a turtle, but I lost
my shell," hissed the creature.

"I will find it!" Rikki said.
Off he went to look.

Rikki looked high and low
for the turtle shell.
Meanwhile, the creature
slipped away.

It was not
a turtle after all!
It was Snake—
and he was heading
for Teddy's house!

The Trick

Snake was curious, too.
He just *had* to know
what was in Teddy's house.
Snake knew he had to
get Rikki out of the way.
Rikki would never let
a snake in the house.

That was a good trick
I played on the mongoose,
Snake thought.
Now, Rikki is busy
looking for a turtle shell—
and I am free to go inside!

Snake went into the pantry.

He made a very big mess.

"This is fun," Snake hissed.

Then he went into the living room.

Snake found Mama's plant.

He curled up in its leaves.

The plant tipped over—

and broke Mama's new lamp.

Mama and Teddy came running.

So did Rikki.
He had not found
the shell that the
creature had lost,

but he had heard
that great big crash.
"I'm coming, Teddy!"
Rikki called.

"Look what Rikki did!"
Mama said to Teddy.
"He didn't!" Teddy said.
"I told him to stay
in the garden."

"Who was it, then?"
asked Mama.
Teddy did not know
what to say.
Neither did Rikki.

The Mongoose Detective

"Rikki *must* have
done this," Mama said.
"Now he cannot come
inside the house."
Rikki was very sad.
He wandered away.
Then he heard crying
from the tall, tall grass,
and he forgot he was sad.
He was curious again!

Rikki crept into
the tall, tall grass.
There he saw the
creature again.

"What is wrong?" asked Rikki.

"You have not found my shell yet!" the creature said. "Won't you help?" Rikki left to search the grass— while the creature slipped away.

This time, though, Rikki saw
the creature slip away . . .
and Rikki was very curious.
He just *had* to know
where it was going!

Rikki followed the creature.

First it lost one leg.

Then it lost another.

Then it lost two more!

This is very strange,
Rikki thought.

Soon Rikki saw who
that creature *really* was.

"It is not a turtle!" Rikki
said. "It is Snake—and he
is going to the house!"

Snake slipped inside
through a hole in the floor
while Mama stood
at the door, sweeping.

Good-bye, Snake

Mama had said Rikki
was not allowed inside,
but the little mongoose
knew he had no choice.
He squeezed into
the hole in the floor.
He had to catch Snake!

Snake was in the pantry.
He was playing with
jars and cans.
"Stop that!" said Rikki.
Snake did not.

Crash!

Smash!

Splat!

They all fell down!

"Get out! Get out!"
Rikki said.

"Catch me if you can,"
hissed Snake.

Rikki chased Snake

around and around.

Rikki ran as fast as he could.

He ran right into Mama!

"Rikki, how could you make this mess?" she asked.

"*Achoo!*" sneezed Snake.

"Look!" said Teddy. "Rikki did *not* make it. Snake made it!"

Mama was surprised.
"It was Snake the
whole time!" she said.
Quick as a wink,
she swept Snake out
of the house . . .

. . . and back into
the tall, tall grass—
which Rikki was never
the least bit curious
about ever again.